Hakari
AND THE GREAT SECRET

Tony Bradman
Karl West

Collins

Contents

Chapter 1
The Great Secret

It had been a busy day in the pet shop. Lots of families had come in to choose a pet, and they had all left looking happy. But one little creature was feeling glum. Nobody had chosen him, and he was beginning to think he would be alone forever.

His name was Hakari, and he was
a young hamster. He'd been part of a family
himself once. Quite a big one, in fact – he'd had
eight brothers and sisters. Yet each of them had
been chosen, and the cage steadily grew more
and more empty.

Now Hakari looked out through the bars and
wondered what to do. Then suddenly it came
to him. He needed some advice, and he knew
just who to ask for it …

Penelope the Parrot was the oldest creature
in the shop, and the one the owner liked best.
Everybody said he would never sell her.

She spent most of the day sleeping on
her perch. But she always took a stroll around
the shop when it closed.

That evening, Hakari listened out for her. After a while, he heard her coming towards his cage, her feet clicking on the floor. Penelope was old, and she was slow. So Hakari knew he would have to be patient. It took ages, but she appeared at last.

"Hey there, Penelope," said Hakari. "Do you mind if I ask you a question?"

"Not at all," she said, coming to a halt. "Although I hope it won't be difficult. My brain is a little slow these days. I suppose that's because I'm so old – "

"I just want to know how to get out of here," said Hakari. "I'd like to be part of a family again. But the humans who come looking for a pet aren't interested in me."

"Ah, I see," said Penelope. "You probably need to catch their attention, look cute and friendly, that sort of thing. But are you sure it's what you truly want?" Penelope tipped her head and frowned, fixing her eyes on Hakari's.

"Yes, I am," said Hakari. "Why do you ask? Is there a problem with that?"

"Perhaps. You're very young, so you might not have heard the stories about what goes on outside this place … You should be careful what you wish for."

"You've got me worried now," said Hakari. The shop was quiet – the only sound was a gentle bubbling coming from the big aquarium. "What do you mean?"

"Oh, let's not go into detail. You'll be fine if you keep your wits about you and remember one thing above all. You must *never* reveal our Great Secret."

"I wouldn't dream of it – although it would help if I knew what it was."

"Seriously? Nobody has ever explained it to you?" said Penelope.

Hakari shook his head, and Penelope gave a deep sigh. "Well, I suppose it's up to me, then … It's quite simple, actually. Humans don't know that we animals understand everything they say, in all their languages. And that if we wanted to, we could talk to them too."

9

"Er … I'm sorry, but I really don't get it," said Hakari, feeling rather puzzled. "That would be a good thing, wouldn't it? Why do we have to keep it such a secret?"

"Oh no, it would be a total disaster if they found out!" Penelope looked horrified. "Probably the end of the world, at least for us animals. Now repeat after me – I swear that I will never give away The Great Secret, cross my paws and hope to die."

It was clearly very important, so Hakari agreed to do as he was told. Penelope was relieved. She wished him luck and carried on with her walk around the shop.

That night, Hakari was so excited he could barely sleep. He was looking forward to the morning. He was going to be the cutest and friendliest hamster *ever* ...

Hamster facts

Hamsters are rodents, so they're related to mice, rats and guinea pigs, as well as squirrels, lemmings and even beavers!

Hamsters have poor eyesight, but very good hearing.

If a hamster mother senses danger, she keeps her babies in pouches inside her mouth!

Those pouches can also be used to store food.

Hamsters can run fast – up to four miles per hour. They can run just as fast backwards as forwards.

There are about 600,000 pet hamsters in the UK alone!

In 1930, a scientist found a family of hamsters in the Syrian desert. All the pet Syrian hamsters alive today are descended from that family!

13

Chapter 2
A bumpy ride

The next day was even busier in the pet shop.
As soon as the owner opened the door,
lots more families came in to choose a pet.
Hakari stood right at the front of his cage.
He watched them all carefully and tried his best
to look incredibly cute and friendly.

After a while, a family of three humans
appeared before him – two parents and their
young son, Hakari realised. They peered at
Hakari in his cage, but it was the boy who came
the closest.

He came right up to the cage and put his face up to the bars.

Hakari thought it was rather scary to see such an enormous creature looming over him. But he didn't back away. He stood up against the bars and looked into the boy's huge brown eyes. He squeaked a lot in a really cute and friendly way, as well.

"I want this one," the boy said.

Fantastic, thought Hakari. *Job done!*
He could hardly believe it had been so easy.

But then the boy's father came closer.
He leaned down and stared hard at Hakari,
clearly studying him much more carefully.
"I don't know, Alfie," said the dad seriously.
"Do you really want another hamster?"

"Your dad's got a point, sweetheart,"
said the boy's mum. "Maybe you should try
something completely different this time.
Perhaps a couple of nice goldfish – "

Oh no, thought Hakari. *So near, yet so far!*

There was only one thing for it – he would just have to be even *more* cute and *more* friendly. But how?

Then he had a brilliant idea. He stretched up on his hind legs, pushed his face right through the cage bars – and touched his nose to Alfie's. It worked instantly.

"No, thanks," said Alfie, smiling. "I really want this hamster … please?"

"Oh, all right then," said his dad. "But don't say we didn't warn you."

Things happened quickly after that. Alfie's mum went to find the owner, and he came over with a carrying cage. Hakari had seen one before. It was a box with a see-through top that was used for transporting small animals to their new homes.

Soon Hakari was being carried out of the pet shop. He discovered that the exterior world was very bright and noisy indeed. But the biggest surprise was that it had no ceiling. Hakari could only see some strange fluffy white shapes high above.

He thought that was scary enough, but there was much worse to come. The carrying cage was put in the back of an enormous metal box on wheels. Everything went dark, there was a loud noise, and Hakari felt it moving beneath him …

It was a bumpy ride, and for a while Hakari wondered if he would survive.

At last, the large metal box seemed to come to a halt. The carrying cage was lifted into the light. It was swung through the air one last time, and finally came to rest.

Alfie gently took Hakari out of the cage. He made a little platform of his hands for the hamster to sit on. Hakari looked round, intrigued. They were in a room full of strange-looking objects, but at least it seemed to have a proper ceiling.

There was *one* thing Hakari recognised – a large cage for a hamster. Alfie lowered his hands in front of its wide-open door. Hakari hopped off and went inside.

"Welcome to your new home, Henry," said Alfie. "That's the name I'm giving you, by the way. Actually, your full name is Henry The Eighth, because I've had seven hamsters before you. I only hope you're going to last longer than the others."

That doesn't sound good, thought Hakari.

Looking after a pet hamster

Hamsters can be a good first pet – they're small and quite easy to care for. Because they are nocturnal, they sleep in the day when you're at school, and they're active at night.

A hamster home

Choose a cage with plenty of space and a lockable door. A cage with different levels is good.

You could add a wheel for the hamster to run on.

Put in some toys like wooden blocks and old toilet roll tubes for it to play with.

Keeping your hamster cosy

Put a thick layer of bedding material in
the bottom of the cage. A box with shredded
paper or cardboard makes a nice spot to
nest in!

Food and drink

Hamsters need a water bottle or dish, and a bowl for their food. You can buy healthy hamster food from pet shops. You can also give them small amounts of greens and tiny pieces of fruit. But don't give them grapes or rhubarb – these can be poisonous for hamsters.

Hamster handling

It's good to let your hamster play outside its cage sometimes, but you need to be there all the time, so it doesn't escape.

Hamsters love being handled, but it's easy to hurt them, so you must be very gentle.

If you're ever worried about your hamster, you should ask a vet for advice.

There's also a lot of information about looking after hamsters online.

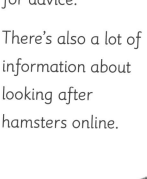

27

Chapter 3
Full of ghosts

Alfie stayed by the cage and chattered away happily for ages. He pointed out all the amazing features of Hakari's new home. It had an exercise wheel, a food bowl, a water bottle, a nice place to sleep, even a mirror.

But Hakari barely listened. He was too busy thinking about the cage's previous inhabitants. For he could tell the cage had been lived in before. There were plenty of dents and scratches, and even a few bent bars.

Seven other hamsters, Hakari kept thinking – that seemed like a lot. He wondered what had happened to them. Maybe they had run away for some reason. But why would they have done that? The cage wasn't great, but it wasn't awful, either.

Then a ghastly thought occurred to him – perhaps they had all died! Now he felt very uneasy.

It was as if the cage was full of ghosts, seven little see-through hamsters squeaking at him … He closed his eyes and tried not to think about it any more.

He managed to calm down after a while. Everything was going to be fine, he kept telling himself. His new cage was actually quite a bit bigger than the old one at the pet shop, so that was OK. Alfie did seem quite nice too, for a human, that is.

Hakari couldn't say the same for Alfie's three sisters. One was called Poppy, and she was older than Alfie. She came to have a look at Hakari in his cage, and pushed Alfie out of the way.

"Hey!", he shouted at her and wheeled back up to the cage.

"Is this one another Henry?" she said. "That's such a stupid name for a hamster!"

Poppy was right, Hakari thought. He didn't much like his new name either, and would have preferred to keep his old one. But he couldn't do anything about it.

Alfie's younger sisters were twins called Darcie and Sienna. They came to see Hakari as well, although they did more than just have a look. They rattled the cage, yelled through the bars, and kept saying they *really* wanted to hold him.

"I don't think so," muttered Alfie. "You'll probably scare him …".

That just seemed to make Darcie and Sienna cross. They both tried to open the cage door, but Alfie pushed their hands away and they started screaming.

Hakari had never heard anything like
it before. The terrible sound cut right
through him.

Alfie's parents came in and took the twins
away, thank goodness. Alfie stayed a while
longer, but then he went off too, and Hakari
breathed a sigh of relief. So far it had all been,
well, a bit … intense. He needed a few moments
of quiet and calm.

Then suddenly a large black dog came trotting into the room and right up to the cage. He was followed closely by an old tabby cat, and there was a third creature with them too. A tiny yellow and green bird was standing on top of the dog's head.

They stared at Hakari with solemn faces, and eventually the bird spoke. "We've come to say hello," he warbled. "Er … while there's still time, that is."

"Excuse me?" said Hakari, rather confused. "What are you talking about?"

"Well, if the other hamsters are anything to go by, you won't be around for very long," said the cat. "I reckon you've got a day, maybe a couple at the most."

"If you're lucky," the dog said sadly. "You might not even make it to lunch."

"So you're telling me I'm doomed," said Hakari. "And why exactly is that?"

"It's because of Alfie," said the bird. "He's very kind but he's a really, *really* terrible pet owner."

Perhaps coming here hadn't been a good idea after all, thought Hakari …

Chapter 4
Decision time!

"Of course, it hasn't *all* been Alfie's fault," Barry the Budgie was saying. "His parents must take some of the blame as well."

The four animals had told each other their names. The dog was a black Labrador called Ruby, and the cat was called Idris. Hakari had listened with horror as they had told him about the family. It seemed there was constant chaos in the house, with things going wrong all the time.

"Oh, don't get us wrong, they're lovely people," said Idris. "They're just not organised — there's no routine. They can be incredibly loud as well."

"I've noticed that," said Hakari. There had been lots of yelling and crashing and banging. "But you still haven't told me how the other hamsters actually died."

"In all sorts of ways," said Ruby. "For example, one was – "

"Er … you can stop there," said Barry, quickly. "Hakari doesn't need to know all the gory details. The thing that killed them was just Alfie always being very … careless."

"Yes, that's right," said Idris, seriously. "For instance, he often forgot to shut the cage door properly. So that meant some of the hamsters could slip out and get into trouble."

"OK, I get it!" said Hakari. Then something else occurred to him. "Hang on – if it's so dangerous here, how come you three have survived?"

"Age and deep cunning, I suppose," said Barry with a bird-like shrug. "We look after ourselves mostly, too. We certainly try not to rely much on the humans."

"But that's probably a lot more difficult for creatures like you hamsters," said Idris, gloomily. You'd have zero chance of … Hey, watch out, I can hear them coming back! See you later, Hakari … I hope."

Alfie spent the rest of the day with Hakari. He talked to Hakari constantly, took him out of the cage a lot, and put him back in again. He let Hakari run up his arm and sit on his shoulder, and they played together for ages. They even touched noses once more. Hakari had to admit that Alfie was really nice – he certainly seemed to be happy to have a hamster once more.

But Hakari couldn't help feeling rather wary of him. If the other pets in the house had told him the truth, then Alfie might be quite dangerous. Interestingly enough, Hakari noticed that Alfie forgot to close the cage door properly several times ...

41

That evening, after everyone had gone to bed, Hakari sat alone in his cage. It was quiet and still in the house, and the rooms were full of shadows. Somebody was gently snoring, yet Hakari lay awake for hours. He had such a lot to think about.

The question was – should he stay or should he leave? He'd wanted so much to be part of a family again, and he did like Alfie. But he didn't want to end up dead like the seven other hamsters. He didn't want to be worried all the time, either.

Although if he did escape, where could he go? It would just have to be back to the pet shop – he didn't know anywhere else. That was OK; perhaps the owner could sell him to somebody else. Penelope would know if that had ever happened before.

Hakari looked in the mirror, and realised that he had made up his mind.

He took a deep breath, opened the door of the cage, and quickly stepped out. Ahead of him was another door, the big one he had come through when he'd arrived.

Little did he know that what lay beyond it was utterly terrifying …

Chapter 5
Sharp white teeth

The big door was closed, but Hakari saw
it had a smaller door set into it. He had
a vague memory of seeing Idris jump through
the smaller door, so perhaps it had been made
specially for cats. With a bit of luck, it might be
all right for a hamster too.

Hakari saw now that it was slightly ajar, so he scrambled up and gave it a push. The little door flew open and he fell out, tumbling down head over heels. He landed on the ground beyond, as the door flapped backwards and forwards above him.

The noise it made seemed incredibly loud, and Hakari froze, sure that it would wake up Alfie and his entire family. But it didn't, and Hakari relaxed. Or at least he did until he turned round – and saw that he was surrounded by darkness.

Silvery light was coming from a strange object in the sky, and soon Hakari began to see more clearly.

The ground in front of him was flat and covered in bits of green stuff. Beyond that, there were some big things, also covered in green stuff.

He realised now that he had a problem
– it all looked rather different from the way
he remembered. So he'd absolutely no idea which
direction to go in. *Oh well,* he thought, and set
off anyway. He would just have to work it out as
he walked.

Suddenly, he saw the silhouette of a large
creature looming over him, and he froze again.
The silhouette came forward out of the shadows,
into the silvery light. Hakari saw that
the creature had red fur, a bushy tail, a long
snout – and a mouth full of sharp white teeth.

"Well, hello," said the creature, in a smooth,
deep voice. "How lovely to meet you. I am
the legendary Freddie the Fox, your friendly
local predator. And you are?"

"Nice to meet you too – I think. My name is Hakari, and I'm a hamster."

"Ah, how delicious … It's a shame you didn't bring a couple of chums."

"Hang on," squeaked Hakari. "Are you saying you're going to *eat* me?"

"Of course," said Freddie, flicking his tongue out to lick his lips. "You're probably thinking of running away, but trust me, it will be less painful if you stand still – "

Freddie lunged forward, those sharp teeth snapping. Hakari turned and scuttled off, with Freddie in hot pursuit. They ran round for what seemed like ages, Hakari doing lots of dodging and only just managing to keep ahead.

After a while, he realised he was heading back towards the door of the house, and he put on a burst of speed. But Freddie did the same, and Hakari could feel him getting closer, and closer. For a moment, Hakari thought he was doomed … Then he made a final leap through the little door and landed inside.

"I'm impressed," said Freddie, sticking his head through the door. "Creatures like you don't usually get away from me so easily. Ah well, catch you next time."

"Not if I see you first," muttered Hakari. But Freddie had already gone.

Hakari returned to the house and tried to calm down. He was shaking from the tip of his nose to the end of his tail, and he was exhausted too. It was just as dangerous outside the house as it was inside! There didn't seem to be any hope at all.

Eventually, the shaking stopped and he began to think straight. What did he *really* want? He wanted to be part of a family.

This one might have a few faults, but the main problem was Alfie … and then Hakari realised what he had to do.

*He would just have to make Alfie into
a much better pet owner!* Although that would
almost certainly mean breaking the promise
he'd made to Penelope …

Hakari's escape

Chapter 6
The right moment

That night, Hakari found it difficult to
sleep again. He kept worrying about what
Penelope had said. Would it really be the end
of the world if he gave away The Great Secret?

It would certainly be the end of me if I don't, he thought.

The truth was that he didn't really have any choice. But then he realised there might be a safe way of doing it. He just had to make sure he thought it all through before he actually opened his mouth and spoke …

By the time the sun rose in the morning, Hakari was ready. The only problem he had now was finding the right moment. He would need to be completely alone with Alfie; Hakari certainly didn't want anyone else in the family to hear him speak.

His chance finally came late in the afternoon. Poppy was upstairs, and Alfie's dad had gone out with the twins.

Hakari could hear Alfie's mum doing some banging and crashing in the kitchen. Alfie found Hakari on the floor.

"I'm so glad you're still alive!" Alfie whispered. "I was so worried about you, I hardly slept a wink last night. I promise I'll do my best to take care of you."

"I'm very glad to hear it," said Hakari. "I didn't sleep too well myself."

"Oh, I'm sorry – " said Alfie. But then his eyes grew wide and his jaw dropped. "Hold on, did you actually *speak?*" he murmured. "I must be dreaming."

"No, you're not dreaming, Alfie," said Hakari. "I can speak your language, and I can understand everything you say. And there are a few things we need to talk about – "

59

Hakari talked for quite a while, and soon Alfie was listening to him as if a talking hamster was completely natural. Hakari explained The Great Secret, and made Alfie promise to keep it. Then he told Alfie what Ruby, Idris and Barry had said.

"They're right, I have been very careless," said Alfie, looking glum. "I feel so guilty! The trouble is that I don't really know what I'm supposed to do."

"To be honest, I'm not sure myself," said Hakari. "I suppose you could start by trying to be more *careful*. Then we could learn together as we go along."

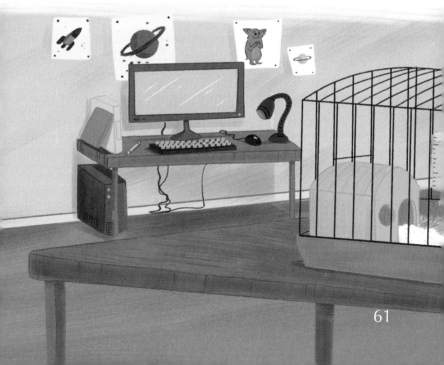

"Umm, that does sound like a plan," said Alfie. "You've given me a brilliant idea now – I should ask Mum and Dad to get me a special book about hamsters."

"If it will help, go for it!" said Hakari. "Although what exactly is a *book*?"

"Oh, books are great," said Alfie, grinning. "I'll show you some. You can find out all sorts of things from them. I don't know why I didn't think of it before."

"Well, there you go," said Hakari, smiling. "You're doing better already."

From then on, with Hakari's encouragement, Alfie made a real effort.

He did ask his mum and dad to get him a book about hamsters, and he spent hours reading it. He kept Hakari's cage clean, and always made sure he had the right food and plenty of water.

He wrote out a list of rules and pinned it to the wall, then made sure everyone stuck to them, especially Darcie and Sienna. They were only allowed to hold Hakari if they were both quiet and gentle with him, and didn't fight with each other.

"There's just one more thing, Alfie," Hakari said, one day. "I hope you don't mind, but I really don't like the name Henry. So could you call me Hakari instead?"

Alfie said he loved the name, and the rest of the family did too, even Poppy. Alfie made a little sign for the cage – *Hakari's House* – and hung it over the door.

Hakari had a feeling he would have a happy life here – and a long one too!

65

Ten fun names for hamsters

 1 Rover

2 Ickle-Sweetums-Darling-Lovey-Pops

 3 Killer

 4 The Ham Man

 5 Henry the Eighth

 6 The Great Hairy Terrifying
Savage Beast

 **7** Harry Kane
(unless your hamster is
a very good footballer).

 8 Tiddles

 9 Guy the Guinea Pig

10 Hammy

Freddie's fox facts

Like hamsters, foxes are nocturnal – they move about at night.

Foxes live in the countryside and in towns.

They like to eat meat, but
will also scavenge food
from bins or eat berries.

Foxes have whiskers
on their legs to help
them feel their way
in the dark.

69

About the author

Why did you want to be an author?

At primary school, my teacher
Mr Smith read our class
The Hobbit by JRR Tolkien and
that got me hooked on reading.
It wasn't long before I decided
I wanted to write stories myself.

Tony Bradman

Why did you decide to write this book?

Years ago on a school visit I met
a boy whose hamster had died that morning! He said
his parents were taking him to buy a new hamster
that evening, and that he was going to call it
Henry the Eighth. That stuck in my mind, and this story
is the result …

What do you hope readers will get out of the book?

Simple – an insight into the world of hamsters, some
idea of what having a pet involves – and lots of fun!

Have you got any pets?

My wife and I have a 12-year-old border terrier called Betty.

If you could pick one animal to have a conversation with, which would you choose? What would you want to ask them about?

It would have to be a humpback whale! We went whale-watching on a holiday years ago and they were amazing! I would just want to ask them – "How does it feel to be so cool?"

If you could have any animal you wanted as a pet, which would you choose?

A small and very demanding border terrier is more than enough for me!

About the illustrator

**What made you want to
be an illustrator?**

As a child I always loved
creating and drawing my own
characters, stories and comic
strips and I knew I wanted
to do this for a job when
I was older.

Karl West

How did you get into illustration?

I sent some of my drawings to some lovely people in
New York called Astound. They get me all my drawing
work now and deal with all the boring paper work.
I just want to draw!

**What did you like best about illustrating
this book?**

I really liked illustrating the characters in the book,
especially the twin sisters.

What was the most difficult thing about illustrating this book?

Alfie's bedroom — there were lots of things to draw.

Is there anything in this book that relates to your own experiences?

I remember being about 7 years old and going to the pet shop with my mum and sister to pick my own pet hamster. He was called Nippy.

Do you have any pets?

I have two very small dogs. One is 6 years old — he is called Chewi. The other is only 10 weeks old and is called Bozworth.

Do you find it easier to draw animals or people? Why?

I find people easier to draw. Sometimes drawing animals doing things people do can be difficult. Especially if they have hooves rather than hands!

Which character in this book was the most fun to draw?

It has to be Hakari!

Book chat

Is there a baddie in this story? Explain your answer.

Did this book remind you of anything you have experienced in real life?

If you could ask the author one question, what would it be?

Which scene in this book stands out most for you? Why?

Which character would you like to talk to? What would you say to them?

Who would you say is the wisest character in the story? Who is the funniest?

Would you like to read a story that follows on from this one? If so, what might be in it?

If you had to give the book a new title, what would you choose?

Do you think any of the characters changed between the start and end of the story? If so, how?

Book challenge:

What's your dream pet and how would you look after it?

Collins
BIG CAT

Published by Collins
An imprint of HarperCollins*Publishers*
The News Building
1 London Bridge Street
London SE1 9GF
UK

Macken House
39/40 Mayor Street Upper
Dublin 1
D01 C9W8
Ireland

10 9 8 7 6 5 4 3 2 1

ISBN 978-0-00-862464-4

British Library Cataloguing-in-Publication
Data
A catalogue record for this publication is
available from the British Library.

Download the teaching notes and
word cards to accompany this book at:
http://littlewandle.org.uk/signupfluency/

Get the latest Collins Big Cat news at
collins.co.uk/collinsbigcat

Author: Tony Bradman
Illustrator: Karl West (Astound Illustration Agency)
Publisher: Lizzie Catford
Product manager and
    commissioning editor: Caroline Green
Series editor: Charlotte Raby
Development editor: Catherine Baker
Project manager: Emily Hooton
Content editor: Daniela Mora Chavarría
Phonics reviewer: Rachel Russ
Copyeditor: Sally Byford
Proofreader: Gaynor Spry
Typesetter: 2Hoots Publishing Services Ltd
Cover designer: Sarah Finan
Production controller: Katharine Willard

Collins would like to thank the teachers and children at
the following schools who took part in the trialling of
Big Cat for Little Wandle Fluency: Burley And Woodhead
Church of England Primary School; Chesterton Primary
School; Lady Margaret Primary School; Little Sutton
Primary School; Parsloes Primary School.

With thanks to Whizz-Kidz for their help in reviewing
this title.

Printed and bound in the UK using 100% Renewable
Electricity at Martins the Printers Ltd

MIX
Paper | Supporting
responsible forestry
FSC
www.fsc.org
FSC™ C007454

This book is produced from independently
certified FSC™ paper to ensure
responsible forest management.

For more information visit:
www.harpercollins.co.uk/green

Acknowledgements
The publishers gratefully acknowledge the permission
granted to reproduce the copyright material in this
book. Every effort has been made to trace copyright
holders and to obtain their permission for the use of
copyright material. The publishers will gladly receive
any information enabling them to rectify any error or
omission at the first opportunity.

p12 & p67 irin-k/Shutterstock, p13 & p68 irin-k/
Shutterstock, p24 Sergei Kolesnikov/Shutterstock, p25
Papilio/Alamy Stock Photo, p26 Lesya Girl/Shutterstock,
p27 Africa Studio/Shutterstock, pp68–69 Eric Isselee/
Shutterstock.